Haunted Castle Tour

Spooky!

At Weasel Towers tonight...

Watch out!
Weasel in ghost costume about!

HUNGRY CROCS IN THE MOAT

£20

LAB RAT

Looking for a keen helper to take part in a very important scientific experiment. Must have an interest in cheese. Apply to Rat's laboratory. 0356713

FAT CAT

Wants new home/owner, preferably with large swimming pool. Only eats caviar from a silver dish. Call Mr Tibbles: 06571-287

E. Weasel: If you are reading this, I want an apology. Shrew.

— MISSING —

4 large, dangerous crocodiles, stolen from the safari park 2 weeks ago. If found do not panic – call Stan's Safari Park.

WEASEL'S AUTOS

Every car is guaranteed to break down as soon as you leave my garage!

USED CARS

MAKE A FORTUNE from others' Misfortune!

GETTING RICH THE easy WAY

Also by the same author:
I'M BETTER THAN YOU!
E. Weasel - An Autobiography

I'M BETTER THAN YOU!

EAT AT WEASEL BURGER

Unhealthy food, terrible service!

C O U P O N

1 for 2

For Hairy Toes,
Furry Paws
and Arthur

This book belongs to:

Evil Weasel ❤ ✱ ESQ

and

KEEP OFF!

EVIL WEASEL
A JONATHAN CAPE BOOK 978 0 224 07091 1

Published in Great Britain by Jonathan Cape,
an imprint of Random House Children's Books
A Random House Group Company

This edition published 2008

1 3 5 7 9 10 8 6 4 2

RANDOM HOUSE CHILDREN'S BOOKS
61– 63 Uxbridge Road, London W5 5SA

www.**kidsatrandomhouse**.co.uk
www.rbooks.co.uk

Addresses for companies within The Random House Group Limited
can be found at: www.randomhouse.co.uk/offices.htm

THE RANDOM HOUSE GROUP Limited Reg. No. 954009

A CIP catalogue record for this book is available from the British Library.

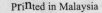

Printed in Malaysia

EVIL WEASEL

Hannah Shaw

JONATHAN CAPE · LONDON

Weasel was evil.

He was a bully and a sneak
– a nasty, measly, evilly Weasel.

His mean schemes and cunning tricks
had made him richer than
you can possibly imagine.

One day Weasel decided to throw a party to boast about his incredible castle, fast car and **huge** swimming pool.

He sent off invitations to everyone he could think of.

invitation

Dear friends,
I, Evil Weasel, invite you —
yes, *you* — to a party.
I am very rich and important,
so don't be late.
Signed,

E. Weasel
ESQ

E. Weasel ESQ. at Weasel Towers
P.S. Watch out, the crocodiles in
the moat might be hungry!

On *the day* of the party
Weasel dressed in his finest clothes
and admired himself in the mirror.

"Don't I look handsome?"
he asked his reflection.

Then Weasel waited expectantly for his guests to arrive.

He waited...

and Waited...

But no one came.

Being rich and powerful isn't much fun when there's no one to impress.

"Why would anyone not want to come to my party?" sulked Weasel.

"I will visit them all and demand an explanation."

First, Weasel went to see Rabbit. He banged on the door.
When Rabbit saw Weasel, he started *shaking*.
"What's the matter with *you*?" said Weasel crossly.
"And why didn't you come to my party?"

Rabbit looked a bit *upset.*

"Don't you remember how *mean*
to me you were at school?"
he asked.

"Oh," said Weasel, *re*membering.

Next, Weasel went to see Rat in his *laboratory*.
"Why didn't you come to my party?"
he snapped.

Rat gulped nervously. He wanted to *run* and hide!

"*B*-because you ruined my *v*-*very* important scientific experiment," he *st*ammered.

"I was just trying to help," lied Weasel.

Off Weasel went to visit Hedgehog, but on the way he met Hedgehog's mum. "Hedgehog isn't *very* well," she said.

"He's been scratching for days and days and he just can't stop."

"Ah," said Weasel, feeling a bit itchy himself.

Weasel was starting to feel quite *guilty*,
so he *crept* past Shrew's house.

"Not so *fast*," said a little voice.

Shrew
Recycling

RECYCLE
MORE!

"It was a joke," protested Weasel.
"My cat only likes caviar,
he wouldn't eat you."

"Well it wasn't funny," squeaked Shrew.

"Nobody came to your party because
you're mean and nasty and a bad friend.
And you never ever say sorry!"

Weasel went *home* feeling m*easly*.
He had been a *h*orrible *bully.*

"I *must fin*d a way to be a *good* friend,"
he thought desperately,

"but h*ow*?"

Weasel paced **rOUnd** and **rOUnd** all night,
trying to think of good ideas.
This wasn't **easy** because
most of *his* thoughts were *wickedly* evil,
but by morning he had a pla*n* . . .

BEING GOOD PLAN

"What *I* need to do," said Weasel,

"is put right everything I've done wrong."

So that is exactly what he did.

Everyone was pleased that Weasel was making *such* an effort.

"But there is still one thing we *haven't* heard you say," said Shrew.

Weasel thought long and hard. After a while, he began to mumble,

"I'm *so . . . so* important! No . . . I'm *su . . .* super e*vil*?"

The other animals began to laugh.

"I've got *it!*" cried Weasel.

"I'm Sorry!"

"Hurray!" they all cheered.

Weasel decided to throw a party
to celebrate being good at being good.

This time, everyone came.

"Yippee!" cried Weasel.

"Let's party!"

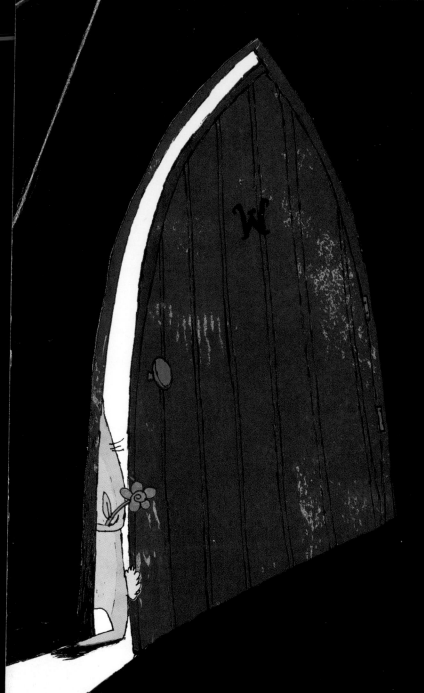

And *I*'d like to say that Weasel *finally* learned
the error of his ways and stopped being *evil* altogether.

But *sometimes* he just couldn't help himself . . .